Lindy Blues

The Missing Silver Dollar

by Dorian Cirrone

illustrated by Liza Woodruff

Marshall Cavendish

For Siena
—D.C.

For Audrey, with love and many thanks
—L.W.

Text copyright © 2006 by Dorian Cirrone
Illustrations copyright © 2006 by Marshall Cavendish

Marshall Cavendish Corporation
99 White Plains Road, Tarrytown, NY 10591
www.marshallcavendish.us

Library of Congress Cataloging-in-Publication Data
Cirrone, Dorian.
The missing silver dollar / by Dorian Cirrone ; illustrated by Liza Woodruff.—1st ed.
p. cm. — (Lindy Blues)
Summary: Fourth-grader and local reporter Lindy investigates the whereabouts of a
silver dollar that has supposedly gone missing from her young neighbor's bank.
ISBN-13: 978-0-7614-5284-3
ISBN-10: 0-7614-5284-2
[1. Reporters and reporting—Fiction. 2. Mystery and detective stories.]
I. Woodruff, Liza, ill. II. Title. III. Series.
PZ7.C499Mis 2006
[Fic]—dc22
2005024721

The text of this book is set in Souvenir.
The illustrations are rendered in pencil.

Printed in The United States of America
A Marshall Cavendish Chapter Book
First edition
2 4 6 5 3 1

Marshall Cavendish Children

Contents

Reporter Lindy Blues here,
Your Nose for News. I sniff out the news. I bring you the news. If there is no news, I make it up.

Just kidding.

Lindy Blues brings you the story behind the story. The story in front of the story. The story beside the story. Well, you get the picture—the whole story.

Here's the scoop on my latest case.

One

A Call from the White House

It's Saturday and the telephone at LBN, the Lindy Blues Network, wakes me up early. It's a news tip. A voice at the other end tells me there's been a robbery at the World Bank. If I want the story I have to be at the White House in thirty minutes. That's the White House on 14th and Flamingo, the home of Joshua Becker.

Fortunately, the LBN office is also my bedroom. I quickly change from my pajamas to my Lindy Blues Fourth Grade Investigative Reporter suit. The pink one with the dark brown shirt that matches my hair. Looking good on camera is a must for any reporter these days.

Besides, when LBN airs tonight at six on the old VCR in the garage, who knows what famous people might be there among my usual neighborhood audience?

I race to find my photographer, Alex, who happens to be my little brother. Since his office is also his bedroom, I find him sleeping. "Wake up," I say. "We've got a story to cover."

Alex rubs his eyes and starts to get ready. Slowly. Alex is a good photographer but he doesn't seem to get that deadlines are important. He changes his clothes and brushes his teeth, but forgets to comb his hair, which is okay because Alex works behind the camera, not in front of it. Like me.

I grab a granola bar and a glass of milk. I wait for Alex to pack up his camera. It's one of those old camcorders that still uses big videotapes for recording and playing, a hand-me-down after Dad went digital and got one that hooks up to the computer.

When Alex is done zipping his camera bag, he stuffs Billy the Beaver and an extra tape into a side compartment. He never leaves home without an extra tape—or Billy the Beaver. Alex acts very old about some things—like math and spelling and being a photographer. But other times he acts like the eight-year-old kid that he really is.

Finally, Alex begins to eat his breakfast. He is a very slow eater. Mainly because he eats his food in alphabetical order—one food at a time. Banana, cereal, milk, orange juice. Today it's apple juice, butter, jelly, toast. Yuck.

I tell him his food would be better mixed together.

He jumps up and down. "There," he says. "Now it's mixed." Normally Alex is very quiet. I think I like him better that way.

When he's through jumping, Alex slings his camera bag over his shoulder. I grab a pen, my reporter's notebook, and my portable microphone. It's not a real mic, but I like my Saturday night broadcasts to look professional.

Finally, we head to the White House.

On the way, Mrs. Carlucci drives by. I wave to her. She does not wave back. Mrs. Carlucci used to be a big fan of the Lindy Blues Network—until a few weeks ago. That's when she heard I did a story about how her cabbage soup diet didn't appear to be working because her dress looked a little bit tighter than usual.

At the same time, I reported there was a funny smell coming from the Carlucci household. Like smells, sometimes news travels very fast. When Mrs. Carlucci got a whiff of the story from some of my usual Saturday night audience of friends and fans, she was not happy. Since then, she does not wave to me or the LBN crew.

That's when I learned that not everyone is a fan of the truth in news reporting.

When we get to the White House, Joshua,

a fellow fourth grader, and his seven-year-old sister, Amy, are waiting outside.

Alex rolls the tape. I put my face between the freckled faces of Joshua and Amy and look straight at the camera. I tap the mic twice and yell, "Is this thing on? Testing one, two, three," because people with real microphones do that all the time.

"This is the LBN news team reporting to you live from the White House. Mr. Becker, tell us about the robbery at the world . . . What?!?! Wait a minute. Stop the tape! Stop the tape! What is going on here?"

I've noticed that Amy is holding a small bank in the shape of, you guessed it—a globe. "Is this the World Bank you were talking about? You call Reporter Lindy Blues away from the rest of the world news to cover a robbery from a plastic bank, a piggy bank—as in *oink oink*? This is an outrage!"

"Calm down," Joshua says. "We're talking about silver dollars here. Amy has been collecting them since she was born.

Yesterday she had eleven dollars in her bank. But this morning, when she woke up, she only had ten dollars."

"So, Mr. Becker," I say, "what we are talking about here is the theft of one dollar?"

"Yes," Joshua says. "But silver dollars can be very valuable, especially the older ones."

"Is Ms. Becker's missing silver dollar an older one?"

"Well . . . no," Joshua answers. "But someday it will be."

At this point I cannot believe that I, Lindy Blues, am covering the theft of one, as in solo, single, *uno* silver dollar. But then again, it has been a slow news week and I do need a good story for tonight's show.

"Okay," I say. "Alex, roll the tape."

Two

Opposite Day

"I'm here at the White House to cover a theft, the theft of a rare and priceless silver dollar." I turn toward Amy. "Ms. Becker, exactly what does this costly coin look like?"

Amy sticks her tongue out of the side of her mouth and looks up at the sky. "It was round and shiny and silver."

"Yes," I say. "I might have guessed that. Can you tell us any more details?"

Amy thinks. "There was a picture of a woman on one side."

"And just who was this woman?" I ask.

"I'm not sure," Amy says. "She had a man's name."

"Hmmm," I say, "a man's name." I have an aunt named Roberta and we call her Rob. And Mrs. Carlucci's name is Josephine and they call her Jo. "Is it Rob or Jo?" I ask.

Amy shakes her head. "I remember now. It's Susan."

"Susan?" I say. "Susan is not a man's name."

Joshua finally chimes in. "It's not her first name that's a man's name. It's her last name. It's Susan B. Anthony."

I make a note to myself: Amy Becker is not the best at giving clues.

I turn toward the camera. "Susan B. Anthony is one of Lindy Blues's personal heroes. She was a champion of women's rights and helped change the law so that women in this country could vote."

I turn back toward Amy. My public service announcement on women's history is over. I'm ready to continue my story. "Ms. Becker, are all of the dollars in your bank Susan B. Anthony dollars?"

"I have one five-dollar bill and all the rest are silver dollars."

"And when did you first notice that this silver dollar was missing?"

"This morning," Amy says. "I woke up, washed my hands and face, then had a bowl of cereal with Rocky Road ice cream on top."

The investigative reporter in me finds this a little bit strange. "You had *what* for breakfast?"

"Cereal and ice cream," Amy says. "I eat it every morning."

I think, perhaps, I should be investigating Amy's eating habits instead of her lost coin. But I let it go. A good journalist stays with the story, no matter what.

"So then what did you do, Ms. Becker?"

"I brushed my teeth and put on my clothes. Then I took the money out of my bank to count it. And I only had ten dollars."

"You were missing one?"

"Yes."

"And how can you be sure that you had eleven dollars in the first place?"

"Because I counted my money yesterday morning."

"Do you count your money every morning, Ms. Becker?"

"No, of course not. That would be greedy. I counted it yesterday because I lost a tooth."

Reporter Lindy Blues is trying to understand the connection between the missing tooth and the missing dollar, but there doesn't seem to be one. "Tell me more," I say.

"I knew the Tooth Fairy would bring me a silver dollar last night because that's what she gave me when I lost my other front tooth. See?" Amy points to the large gap in her teeth. "So, I wanted to know how much I would have when she gave me the new dollar."

"Okay," I say. "Let's go over yesterday's

events. You woke up, washed your hands and face, and had cereal and ice cream."

"No, I did not," Amy says. "I had a hamburger and French fries."

"But I thought you said you have cereal and ice cream every morning."

"Nope," Amy says, "not yesterday. Yesterday was Opposite Day."

"Opposite Day?"

"Yes," Joshua says. "Opposite Day is when you do everything opposite all day long. You know, like eat dinner in the morning and breakfast at night."

"Okay," I say. "Just who started this Opposite Day thing?"

"My summer camp counselor," Amy says.

"Perhaps this camp counselor had something to do with your missing silver dollar," I say.

Suddenly, Amy starts crying.

I tell Alex to turn the camera away from her face. My audience should not see that I made a child cry.

Amy is whispering something in Joshua's ear.

"What's wrong?" I ask.

Joshua puts his face in front of the camera and shouts. "Amy wants everyone to know she loves her camp counselor."

"Very well," I say. "Then where did this camp counselor get the idea for Opposite Day?"

Amy sniffles. "From TV, Channel 35."

I shake my head. Why can't people just stick to the Lindy Blues Network?

Three

Rockin' Rockets

I am about to ask another question, but suddenly I feel a breeze behind me. Could this be a clue? I turn around. Joshua Becker is jumping up and down. Up and down.

I stare at him. I remember that Alex did the same thing earlier. "Breakfast?" I ask.

"No, thank you," he says. "I already ate."

It's no use explaining. "Why are you jumping up and down?" I ask.

Joshua's hair flies up like the hair of a cartoon character falling off a cliff. Then it flops down on his head. "I'm practicing," he says.

"For what?" I ask. "A Mexican jumping bean contest?"

"No," Joshua says. "But you're right about the contest part."

Lindy Blues is all ears. My viewers love to hear about contests. Last week the Lindy Blues Network covered a blueberry pie-eating contest. Amy Becker was the winner. In fact, the tip of her nose is still slightly blue.

I decide to switch from the silver dollar story for a minute.

"Tell me about this contest, Mr. Becker," I say.

Joshua stops jumping. He is out of breath. "It's a Rockin' Rocket Contest," he says between loud pants. He sounds a lot like his golden retriever, Dakota, who is mysteriously absent from this interview.

Joshua starts jumping again. I move my head up and down. Up and down. "So Mr. Becker, exactly what is involved in this so-called Rockin' Rocket Contest? Could it be a . . . *rocket*?"

"Well, duh, Lindy, um, I mean Ms. Blues," he says.

Joshua knows that when we are on camera my name is Ms. Blues. But he does not seem to know that saying "duh" to a reporter on camera is also against the rules. I decide to let it go this time and continue my questions.

"Exactly who is participating in this contest, Mr. Becker?"

Joshua gets a serious look on his face and stops jumping. He points toward his next-door neighbor's house. "It's between me and Will Malone."

Lindy Blues knows about the competitive spirit between Joshua Becker and Will Malone. "And just how will this rocket contest work?" I ask.

"Will and I are going to see whose rocket goes up higher in the air," Joshua says. "The one that goes the highest wins."

"Hmm, Mr. Becker. May I ask what kind of rocket you are using for this contest?"

"It's made out of rubber and plastic. There's a balloon you jump on that makes the rocket shoot up in the air."

I put the microphone close to Joshua's face. "And just how much did you have to pay for this rocket, Mr. Becker? Could it have been one dollar? One *silver* dollar?"

"Lindeeee," Joshua shouts. "Do you really think I'd steal from my own sister? I mean, she's a pain sometimes, but I'd never steal from her. Besides, I got the rocket for a birthday present. Last Tuesday."

Suddenly I remember. The Lindy Blues Network did cover a birthday celebration at the Becker household last week. I write in my reporter's notebook: "Review tapes to see if Joshua Becker received a rocket for a present."

I am beginning to realize that this silver dollar mystery might turn into a silver dollar nightmare for the Lindy Blues Network. If I can't find the coin, the rocket contest might have to be my top story. I smile at Joshua in an attempt to make up for suggesting he is a suspect. "Well then, Mr. Becker. May we see this rocket?"

Joshua runs to the back of his house and waves to me and my crew to follow him. We trudge through the weeds to the Becker's backyard. I make another note in my reporter's notebook: "Possible news story: Weeds. Are They Taking Over *Your* Neighborhood?"

Joshua points us toward the porch. He pulls out a strange looking contraption. He blows up the balloon part and puts it on the ground. He sticks the red, plastic rocket in a holder attached to the balloon. He begins to count: "Ten, nine, eight, seven, six . . ."

Just as he gets to one, he bends his knees way down and jumps slightly off the ground. He lands on the balloon and yells, "Blast off!"

The rocket does not seem to have heard him. Instead of blasting off, it has gone something like, "Pffft!"

Amy stares at the rocket, which is lying in the grass. For a minute, she forgets about her dollar. "Too bad it still isn't Opposite Day," she says. "You'd win the contest for sure."

Four

Miranda Malone, Secret Weapon

Just as Joshua starts to put his rocket back together, another rocket flies through the air, up and over the tall bushes that separate the Becker and Malone backyards. It lands right next to Joshua's feet. He slumps into a nearby lawn chair. "Oh no," he says. "It's over."

"No," I say. "The story is just beginning. We haven't even interviewed all the suspects."

Joshua shakes his head. "I mean the contest. It's over. That's Will Malone's rocket. I can't compete with that."

"What do you mean?" I say. "You're giving up already? What if Lindy Blues decided to give up? What if LBN decided to close its offices because it was too hard to find news stories? Where would you be then?"

Amy looks up at me and smiles. "Right here in the backyard?"

Just as I am about to remind her about the missing silver dollar, Will Malone strolls toward us. His sister, Miranda, follows him. She is not strolling. She never strolls. She is traveling the way only Miranda Malone travels—cartwheels, flips, hand springs, crab walks. Anything but plain old steps.

"Has anyone seen a rocket?" Will asks.

Joshua points. "Over there."

"Funny," Will says. "There's your rocket on the ground, but I never saw it in the air."

Joshua is silent.

Everyone else is silent. Then Amy breaks in. "You must have been looking the other way."

Joshua smiles and gets up from the chair. "That's right," he says, pointing to the resting rocket. "Because this is a great rocket. A rockin' rocket. A rocket that'll beat your rocket any day of the week!"

Will Malone looks at his watch. "Well, the Rockin' Rocket Contest is in exactly two hours. Then we'll see." He picks up his rocket and strolls out of the yard. Miranda flip-flops behind him, her blond ponytail whooshing in the wind.

I notice that my photographer is filming Miranda instead of me. "Hey," I say. "Remember me, Lindy Blues, Your Nose for News." Alex's face turns red.

Amy looks up at Joshua. "So, Mr. Rocket Man, what are you going to do now?"

Joshua slumps back into the chair. "I have no idea."

I get out my reporter's notebook and write down the time of the rocket contest. When I look up, my photographer is nowhere in sight. Suddenly, I hear, "Psssst." I turn toward the sound. Alex is holding his camera between the leaves of the bushes.

"Alex," I say. "We have already done a story on the Malones' overgrown hedges."

"Shhh," he says, motioning for us to join him.

Joshua and I tiptoe toward the bushes. We poke through them to see the Malones' backyard. Spying is not something Lindy Blues likes to do. But sometimes it is necessary in order to find out the real story.

On the other side of the bushes, a distance away, we see Will and Miranda Malone. We watch as Will Malone blows up a balloon and attaches it to the rocket holder. He then motions to Miranda to move away. We can see his lips counting. "Ten, nine, eight, seven, six . . ." as she walks backward to the fence. He continues to count and Miranda begins to run. She approaches the rocket. She does a huge flip. She lands—Smack!—right on the balloon. The rocket bursts into the air, zooming up through the sky about fifteen feet.

"Wow!" Amy says.

"Did you see that?" Alex asks.

Joshua pulls his head out of the bushes and brushes a leaf from his hair. "So *that's* how he does it."

"Yes," I say. "It's simple. Height plus weight equals . . . well, WHAM!"

I look back through the bushes at Miranda Malone. I make a note to myself that Will and Miranda Malone are very sneaky neighbors. Then I look at Joshua's frowning face. "Don't worry. Lindy Blues will think of something. But first, we have a missing silver dollar to find. Ms. Becker, where were we?"

"I was eating my dinner for breakfast," she says.

"Yes, that's right," I say. "Opposite Day. So, Ms. Becker, you ate your dinner, then what?"

29

"While I was eating, I felt something funny in my mouth."

"Your tooth?"

"No," she says, "one of those little hard things you sometimes find in hamburgers."

At this point, my stomach feels queasy. "Could we skip the dinner details and get on with it?"

Amy makes two fists and puts them on her hips. "I'm just trying to tell you what happened."

"Please," I say. "Go on."

"On the next bite of my hamburger, my tooth came out. I washed it and put it in a plastic bag."

"And put it on top of your pillow?" I ask.

"No, of course not," Amy says. "I put it *under* my pillow."

"But I thought it was Opposite Day," I say. "If it was Opposite Day, shouldn't you have put your tooth on top of the pillow?"

"No, silly," Amy says. "The Tooth Fairy wouldn't have known it was Opposite Day."

I am beginning to lose my patience with this

story. But I remember it is August, a slow news month. "Okay," I say. "Then what did you do?"

"I opened my bank and counted my money to see how much I would have when I got my new silver dollar."

"And how much was in the bank?"

"I told you—eleven dollars."

"Now, Ms. Becker. I want you to think carefully. Are you sure that when you counted the money you didn't add the silver dollar that you planned on getting from the Tooth Fairy?"

"I'm positive," Amy says.

Suddenly, I remember something. "By the way," I say. "Where is the new silver dollar?"

"I don't have it," Amy says. "The Tooth Fairy forgot to come."

Somehow this doesn't surprise me. I am getting the idea that the Becker house is not your average household.

"I'm sure the Tooth Fairy will come tonight," Joshua says, giving me a wink.

Amy smiles.

31

Five

Searching for Suspects

"Okay," I say. "Let's get back to the money. Yesterday, you counted it and you had eleven dollars. What did you do with the money after you counted it?"

"I put it back in my bank," Amy says.

"Are you sure? Are you sure you didn't drop one of the silver dollars?"

"I don't think so," Amy says. "I would have heard the clink on the floor."

"Not really," I say. "It could have fallen on the bed or somewhere else. Do you mind if we search your room?"

"No," Amy says. "Follow me."

We go to Amy's room. No surprises. It's a mess. Candy wrappers on the floor. Popcorn boxes on the bed. Popsicle sticks on the dresser. "Yuck," I say, forgetting that a good reporter has to keep her opinions to herself. "How can you find anything in here?"

"I know exactly where everything is," Amy says.

This is hard to believe.

Amy walks around the room. She looks under the candy wrappers. She looks under the popcorn boxes. She does not look under the Popsicle sticks. They are too small to hide anything. Besides, they are stuck to her dresser.

"I don't see any silver dollars," Amy says. "I'm sure I put them all back in the bank."

"Okay," I say, turning to Joshua. "Mr. Becker, I'd like to continue my search. Which way to your bedroom?"

"What? I told you I would never steal money from my own little sister!"

"Calm down, Mr. Becker. You know a

good reporter must leave no room for mistakes. Get it? *Room*. Bedroom. Room for mistakes." Sometimes a bit of humor helps in a situation like this.

"Of course, I don't think you stole from your sister," I say. "But, perhaps somehow the silver dollar could have been, shall we say, misplaced."

"Oh, all right," Joshua says.

Whew! A good reporter has to think fast. Amy, Alex, and I follow Joshua to his room.

As Joshua searches the room, I hear a jingling under the bed. I know that sound. It is the sound of coins clanking together. My heart starts pounding. I am about to solve the mystery. Slowly, I lean over and look underneath the bed. Then . . .

"Dakota!" Joshua yells. "I was wondering where you were."

I take a look at the Beckers' dog. She is wearing a dog collar—a perfect place to hide a silver dollar.

"Aha!" I say. "Another suspect." I point
to Dakota. "Look. Around her neck."

Amy starts to cry. Alex knows by now to
turn the camera away.

"No way," Joshua says.

I look closer. It's true. No coin. Only her
license and dog tag. But Dakota is still a
suspect. Everyone is a suspect.

"Where was Dakota when this coin disappeared?" I ask.

"Lindeeeee," Joshua says. "Dakota is not a thief."

"Maybe not," I say. "But have you noticed anything different about Dakota? Her eating habits? Is she fond of round, shiny objects?"

Amy reaches over and strokes Dakota's long, golden fur. "My mom only lets Dakota eat dog food. She's not even allowed to have table scraps. And speaking of table scraps, I'm hungry. Isn't it time for lunch?"

I look at my watch. "Alex," I say, "you can stop the tape."

Lindy Blues could use a little lunch herself. I've got a rocket contest to cover and a missing silver dollar to investigate. All in a few hours.

Six

Brett Dot Com

When I get back to LBN headquarters, I contact my research department. My research department is in the bedroom of my big brother, Brett. Or, as I call him, Brett Dot Com. He's a computer whiz, and he hates it when I call him by his nickname.

"Hey, Shorty," he says, without taking his eyes off the computer screen. "Get outta my room."

Sometimes research departments can be very uncooperative.

"The Lindy Blues Network needs some facts. Can I count on you?"

"No."

"Well, then I guess LBN will have to use another story on tonight's broadcast. Maybe my report on the sleeping habits of teenage boys."

Brett stops looking at the computer screen. "What report?"

"Oh, it's a little something Alex and I covered while you were sleeping. By the way, did you know that nine out of ten teenage boys drool in their sleep? I think that's something Kristin Carlucci would find interesting. She's a cheerleader at your school, isn't she? And a big fan of the Lindy Blues Network."

Kristin Carlucci is not *exactly* a big fan of LBN. But ever since the cabbage-soup broadcast, her mother sends her to my garage every Saturday night to make sure there's no more news about the Carlucci family.

Brett closes the window on the computer. "Okay," he says. "What do you need to know?"

"Everything you can find out about silver dollars."

Brett does a search and clicks the mouse a few times. Pictures of silver coins appear.

"There are a few kinds of silver dollars. Which one do you want to know about?" Brett says.

"Susan B. Anthony dollars," I say.

Brett clicks the mouse a few more times. A picture of a Susan B. Anthony dollar appears alongside a couple of long paragraphs. Brett begins reading.

"'Susan B. Anthony was the first real-live woman to be pictured on a United States coin. The dollars were used from 1979 to 1981. People didn't like the coins because they looked too much like quarters.'"

"Whoa, hold on," I say. It's a good thing Brett is a computer whiz. He will never be an announcer with the Lindy Blues Network.

He talks way too fast. And he refuses to wear a tie.

"There's one more thing," he says. "Susan B. Anthony dollars were also produced in 1999 for snack machines and subways."

"Hmmm," I say. "Amy Becker and snack machines go together like Lindy Blues and the news."

"Yeah," Brett says. "Whatever." That is another reason why Brett will never be on the LBN news team. He does not care about clues.

"Here are some more facts for your news show," Brett continues. "'In 2000, a new dollar coin replaced the Susan B. Anthony dollar. It's the same size as the Susan B. Anthony dollar, but it's gold-colored and there's a picture of a famous Indian woman named Sacagawea on it.'" Brett closes the information on the screen and turns to me. "That enough information for you, Shorty?"

I try not to get upset that a famous news person like me has to put up with a nickname like Shorty. "Yes," I say. "Thank you very much."

Seven

Weighing the Facts

Back at the LBN office, I review last Saturday's broadcast. Joshua Becker did have a birthday party last week. And he did get a rocket for a present. He is no longer a suspect.

I take out my notebook and write down the facts.

1. Amy had eleven silver dollars yesterday. But today she has ten.
2. Amy was supposed to get a silver dollar from the Tooth Fairy. But the Tooth Fairy didn't come.
3. Susan B. Anthony silver dollars look a lot like quarters.

4. Dollar coins are used in snack machines.
5. Yesterday was Opposite Day. But today isn't.

I review the list. There are five facts. But are they all clues? I look at my watch. A half hour until the rocket contest.

I join Alex in the kitchen. Mom has made him his version of a peanut-butter-and-jelly sandwich—two slices of bread, a blob of jelly, and a blob of peanut butter. He has already eaten the bread and the jelly. Now he is working on the peanut butter. It's a good thing water begins with "W." Alex is going to need it to wash everything down.

Mom has made me the same thing, but not in separate piles. "Thanks," I say. "The LBN cafeteria is the best."

Mom frowns for a second, then smiles. "Just make sure you remember the cafeteria help when you're rich and famous."

I tell her I'm already famous, but she's not listening. She's filling up Alex's water glass—for the third time. "You're going to float away if you drink anymore," she says.

Alex swallows.

"Not really," I say. "He'll just keep getting heavier and heavier."

Mom nods. "Yes, I guess you're right."

I take a bite of my sandwich. Then I get an idea. Lindy Blues is always on the job—even during lunch time. "Mom," I say. "How much do you think Amy Becker weighs?"

"Hmm," she says. "Maybe about fifty pounds."

"Do you think Amy Becker weighs more or less than Miranda Malone?"

Mom thinks for a minute. "Miranda is a little bit taller. But Amy is a little bit, well . . . you know. I think they weigh about the same."

"Great," I say. "Can I get a thermos of water and my winter coat with all the pockets?"

Her eyes open wide. "First you ask me how much Amy and Miranda weigh and now you want to wear your coat when it's more than ninety degrees outside? What's going on?"

I open the cabinet and pull out the thermos. "Can't explain. Gotta hurry."

I fill up the thermos while my mother gets the coat. Thank goodness she understands the importance of an investigative reporter's job. There are some questions that can't be answered when you're in a hurry.

Alex is almost through drinking. "C'mon," I say. "We've got a Rockin' Rocket Contest to cover." I shove the thermos under my arm and grab the coat. "Thanks, Mom," I say. "See you at six in the garage."

When Alex and I return to the Beckers' house, Joshua and Amy are in the backyard. Joshua is frowning and looking down at his rocket, which has just gone Pffft! once again. Then he looks up at me. "What's with the thermos and coat?"

As an investigative reporter, I am not supposed to care who wins the contest. But because Joshua is my friend, I've decided to bend the rules. "These," I say, holding up the thermos and coat, "are your ticket to Rockin' Rocket stardom."

Joshua and Amy look puzzled.

I hand Amy the thermos.

She takes off the cap and sniffs. She wrinkles her nose. "It's just water."

"I know," I say. "But if you want to be a Rockin' Rocket star, you've got to drink the whole thing."

Amy thinks for a second, then begins to drink. One thing I have learned in the news business: Everyone wants to be a star.

I hand Amy the coat. She puts it on and finishes what's in the thermos. Then I tell her, "Go get your bank."

She starts to protest. But I bring up the star thing again. Amy goes inside.

When she returns with the bank, I start shaking the money out of it.

"What are you doing?" she screams.

"You need to put your money in the two coat pockets," I say. "Remember, height plus weight equals . . . WHAM!"

"There you go again," Joshua says. "What does that mean anyway?"

"Simple," I say. "Amy and Miranda weigh about the same amount. But if Amy drinks this water and adds the extra weight of the silver dollars and the coat, she'll weigh more than Miranda."

"I see," Joshua says. "So more weight on the rocket balloon will make the rocket fly higher."

I smile. "That's right!"

Joshua wrinkles his brow. "But if height plus weight equals WHAM! . . . where are we going to get the height? Amy can't flip like Miranda."

50

This is true. No one can flip like Miranda. I look around the yard. Amy is counting her money on the big, wooden picnic table. "Aha!" I yell.

Joshua jumps away from me.

I point to the table. "Amy can stand on that and jump on the balloon."

Joshua smiles. "Now that's a plan."

Meanwhile, Amy has spread her money on top of the table. She makes a row of silver dollars and puts her five-dollar bill next to them. She leans over and sticks her tongue out of the side of her mouth. Slowly, she begins to count. "One . . . two . . . three . . . four . . . five." Then she draws an imaginary plus sign on the table between the five silver dollars and five-dollar bill. "Five silver dollars plus a five-dollar bill equals ten dollars," she says, clearly proud of her addition skills.

"That's great," I say. "Now put those silver dollars in your pockets. And the bank too. It's Rockin' Rocket time!"

Eight

The Contest

Soon a crowd is assembled in the Beckers'
backyard. Will Malone has apparently invited
the whole neighborhood to watch him. I
recognize many of the faces from my Saturday
night broadcasts. I wave and smile at my fans.

Suddenly I realize this is a good opportunity
to search for more suspects in my missing
silver dollar case. I roam through the crowd
with my microphone. I surprise a few people
when I shout in their faces, "And where were
you yesterday when Amy Becker's silver dollar
mysteriously disappeared?"

They all seem to have alibis.

Then I look at Will and Miranda Malone. Because their mother is a friend of Joshua's mother, I know for a fact that Will and Miranda are always in and out of the Becker house.

I whisper to Joshua. "When did you first hear about the rocket contest?"

"Yesterday," Joshua says. "Why?"

"Aha!" I whisper.

Joshua jumps back.

I make a note to myself: Do not whisper "Aha!" to Joshua Becker when you are trying to have a secret conversation.

I whisper my theory. "Could Will Malone have taken the silver dollar when he came over to tell you about the rocket contest?"

Joshua shakes his head.

"How can you be so sure?" I whisper.

"Because Will didn't come over to tell me about the contest. Miranda did."

I start to whisper, "Aha!" when I remember my new rule. I turn the "ha" into a "choo" and fake a sneeze.

Joshua jumps back anyway.

I make another note to myself: Do not sneeze in front of Joshua Becker when you are trying to have a secret conversation.

"Could Miranda have stolen the silver dollar?" I whisper.

Joshua shakes his head and points to a flipping Miranda. "Look at her," he whispers. "She could never hide anything in her pockets. It would fly right out."

He has a point.

Meanwhile, the crowd is getting restless. They are anxious for the contest to start. Alex puts in his spare tape and turns the camera toward me. I begin my broadcast.

"We are here in the Beckers' backyard for a great event. A rockin' event. On my right I have Joshua Becker with his assistant, Amy Becker. On my left is Will Malone and his assistant, Miranda Malone."

Joshua and Will draw straws to see who will begin the contest. Will picks the long straw and decides to go first. He blows up the balloon part of the rocket and motions for Miranda to move far away. Just like before, he begins to count. Miranda runs toward the balloon. Flips. Lands. And WHAM! The rocket flies about fifteen feet in the air.

"Hah!" Will Malone says into the camera. "Let's see Joshua Becker beat that!"

Joshua looks nervous. He is pacing back and forth. Amy is sweating—not because she is nervous, but because she is wearing a winter coat in ninety-degree weather.

Joshua takes a deep breath and blows up the balloon. Amy stands there sweating.

I look at Miranda Malone. She is very thin. I suspect she will never need the cabbage-soup diet. Or any other diet.

I look at Amy again. With the coat, the silver dollars, and the bank, plus all the water she drank, we've got the weight thing covered. Now for the height.

Amy climbs onto the table. Joshua begins to count, "Ten, nine, eight, seven, six . . ."

When he gets to one, Amy jumps and lands
on the balloon. WHAM!

The rocket blasts into the air like fireworks.
It blasts so high that it lands on the roof.

The crowd cheers. Even though there is
no way of measuring, it is clear that Joshua
is the winner.

Joshua jumps up and down shouting. "Yay!"

Will yells something about a rematch.

Miranda starts a round of back flips.

Alex turns the camera toward Miranda.

And Amy keeps sweating.

But Lindy Blues remembers she has a job to do. I make my announcement to the crowd. "You are all invited to watch this spectacular event once again, tonight on my news show at the LBN studio. For those of you who aren't already Lindy Blues fans, the LBN studio is also known as . . . my garage. In addition, I will be presenting my investigative report on a very valuable missing silver dollar. Tune in at six."

As the crowd breaks up, I look around for Alex. He is still filming Miranda Malone. I let him continue. We can use the tape as filler on a slow news day.

Behind me I hear sobbing. I spin around to find Amy Becker. She is sobbing and sweating.

"What's wrong?" I ask. "Aren't you happy your brother won the contest? Aren't you happy that I made you a star?"

"Waaaahhh," Amy continues to cry. "You still didn't find my silver dollar."

"That's right," Joshua says. "We never found Amy's silver dollar." I can tell he is trying not to sound too happy about winning the Rockin' Rocket Contest.

"Don't worry," I say. "They don't call me Nose for News for nothing. Wow. That's a tongue twister. I make a note never to try to say that on camera.

Amy stops sniffling. I help her off with my coat so she can stop sweating. "Lindy Blues has not forgotten the missing silver dollar," I say. "Stay tuned to the six o'clock news when I will broadcast the results of my investigation."

"Okay," Amy says.

"And you'll broadcast the rocket contest, too, right?" Joshua asks.

"Yes," I say. Then Alex and I hurry home. We hurry because even though I have promised to broadcast the results of my investigation, I still do not know what happened to the silver dollar.

Nine

The LBN Newscast

Alex and I get ready for the broadcast. But the mystery is still a mystery to me.

I begin to think out loud. "Let's see. Amy had a five-dollar bill and six silver dollars yesterday."

Alex nods while he rewinds the rocket contest tape.

"Today she has only five silver dollars."

He nods again and presses Forward to review the tape.

"All the coins pictured Susan B. Anthony. Susan B. Anthony silver dollars are sometimes confused with quarters and sometimes used in snack machines. The Beckers' dog, Dakota, does not eat snacks. He only eats dog food. Amy Becker eats everything. Yesterday was Opposite Day so she ate dinner in the morning. Today is not Opposite Day so she will eat her dinner tonight."

Alex rewinds the tape again so he can watch Miranda Malone flip one more time.

As I watch Miranda run and Will count, "Ten, nine, eight, seven, six, five . . . ," I get an idea. An idea so good that it seems like it is pounding in my brain.

Through the pounding, I hear Alex's voice. "Lindy," he says. "Someone's knocking."

I raise the garage door to find Amy and Joshua. Amy is holding her bank. Joshua is holding my winter coat.

"Thank you," I say. I'm glad they are early. I have a few more questions for Ms. Becker.

"Alex," I say. "Do you still have the silver-dollar tape in the camera?"

He nods and points the camera toward me.

"Roll it," I say, turning toward Amy.

"Ms. Becker, could you tell me more about Opposite Day?"

"You just do everything opposite," she says.

"Like what?"

"For one thing, you stay in your pajamas all day. You don't put your clothes on until nighttime, before you go to bed."

"After you eat breakfast, right?" I ask.

"Yes, that's it," Joshua says. "And, remember, Amy, you also slept upside down."

"That's right," Amy says. She wrinkles her freckled nose. "That might be why the Tooth Fairy didn't want to come to my pillow. My feet were on it."

This Opposite Day thing is sounding crazier and crazier. But just as I think I have the answer, I realize my audience has begun to trail into the garage.

"Stop the tape," I yell to Alex. "The solution to this mystery will have to wait. It's time for the broadcast."

Once everyone is seated on the garage floor, Alex plays the tape of the rocket contest.

The audience cheers when the rockets blast. They cheer even more when their faces are displayed on the television screen.

When that portion of the broadcast is over, Alex changes the tape. Everyone watches intently, following the mystery of Amy's missing silver dollar. As we reach the end of story so far, Alex freezes the tape on a close-up of Amy's face. The gap between her teeth looks huge.

Now it is time for the live portion of my broadcast. I point to the screen and turn toward the audience. "There you have it, folks. Opposite Day. A missing silver dollar. And a sad little girl. Can *you* solve the case?"

Ten

The Mystery Is Solved

It is clear by the puzzled looks of audience members that they are all stumped.

This is when Lindy Blues Your Nose for News goes into action. "We are here at the LBN studios to solve the mystery of Amy Becker's missing silver dollar. But first, let's bring Ms. Becker up. Ms. Becker did you write anything yesterday?"

Amy turns toward the audience. "Yes, I did."

"May I see it?"

Amy frowns. "I don't have it anymore."

I hand her a piece of paper and a pencil.

"Can you recreate what you wrote yesterday?"

Amy scribbles on the paper and hands it to me. She has written the words "*tac*," "*taf*," "*tam*," and "*tah*."

"What exactly is this?"

"It's the opposite of cat, fat, mat, and hat."

"So," I say. "You did everything backwards yesterday?"

"Yes, I did."

"Ms. Becker, could you bring me your bank?" I ask.

Amy gets the bank from Joshua, who has been guarding it in the audience.

"Please open it."

Amy takes the little plug out of the bank, somewhere near Australia. She places the money on the table. I line up the five silver dollars and put the five-dollar bill next to them.

"Ms. Becker, would you please count the money?"

Amy leans over the table. Her tongue is sticking out of the side of her mouth. She starts with the silver dollars. She counts, very slowly. "One . . . two . . . three . . . four . . . five." Then she draws a plus sign on the table between the five silver dollars and five-dollar bill. "Five silver dollars plus a five-dollar bill equals ten dollars," she says.

Then she adds, "How is this going to help me find my silver dollar?"

There are whispers from the audience. The crowd is getting impatient.

I hold up a finger and shout to the crowd. "Just one more minute and I, Lindy Blues, will solve the mystery of the silver dollar."

I turn back to Amy. "Ms. Becker, now please count your money the way you counted it yesterday, on Opposite Day."

"Okay," Amy says. "But I still don't get how counting my money over and over is going to help."

I smile a confident smile at the audience.

Amy touches her index finger to the silver dollar at the top of the row and counts slowly, just the way I thought she would—backwards.

"Ten . . . nine . . . eight . . . seven . . . six." She draws a plus sign between the silver dollars and the five-dollar bill again and says, "Six plus five equals . . . eleven!"

Amy gasps.

The audience gasps.

I do not gasp.

"You *see*, Ms. Becker, you never had eleven dollars. No one stole your silver dollar. By counting your money the opposite way, you only *thought* you had eleven dollars."

"You mean if it isn't Opposite Day, I only have ten dollars?"

"No," I say. "I mean you only have ten dollars no matter what day it is."

"Are you sure?" Amy says. It is difficult for her to comprehend this imaginary loss of one dollar.

"What if every day is Opposite Day? Then will I have eleven dollars?"

"No, you will not," I say. "You will only have eleven dollars in your mind. That doesn't count."

Amy is starting to sniffle again. I must think fast. The audience is getting restless. "Ms. Becker," I say. "What about that tooth? I'm sure the Tooth Fairy will remember you tonight."

"Yes," Joshua adds from the audience, "especially if you sleep with your head on the pillow and your feet at the other end of the bed."

"That's right," I say. "Then tomorrow you will have eleven dollars."

Amy is quiet for a minute. She smiles her toothless smile. She is happy now. It is time to wrap up my live broadcast.

I turn to the audience. "There you have it. A feel-good kind of story. What could have been a sad tale about the theft of a valuable coin has ended with the solving of a math mystery and a smiling little girl." I point to Amy's face once again.

"This is Lindy Blues, Your Nose for News, signing off. Be sure to join us next Saturday night at six for another exciting broadcast at the LBN studio."

"All right!" someone yells from the crowd.

"Good broadcast, Lindy," another voice shouts.

The crowd begins to break up.

"Thanks," Joshua says. "Even if Amy only has ten dollars, at least we know there isn't a thief in the neighborhood."

Amy stands next to him, clutching the bank under her arm. Just in case Joshua is wrong, she isn't taking any chances with her silver dollars.

Will Malone heads out of the garage with Miranda doing a crab walk behind him.

I go over to Alex to thank him for being a great photographer, as usual. But he is watching Miranda. I make a note for a future story: Miranda Malone—Human Pretzel.

Once everyone is gone, Mom closes the garage door and points toward the kitchen.

"But there's lots more news to cover," I say.

She shakes her head. "Even investigative reporters have to be inside by dark."

Alex and I follow her into the kitchen and call it a night.

This is Lindy Blues, Your Nose for News. Till next time.